STERLING CHILDREN'S BOOKS
New York

An Imprint of Sterling Publishing
387 Park Avenue South
New York, NY 10016

STERLING CHILDREN'S BOOKS and the distinctive Sterling Children's Books
logo are trademarks of Sterling Publishing Co., Inc.
© 2012 by Sterling Publishing Co., Inc.

ISBN 978-1-4027-8335-7 (hardcover)

Library of Congress Cataloging-in-Publication Data Available
Distributed in Canada by Sterling Publishing
c/o Canadian Manda Group, 165 Dufferin Street
Toronto, Ontario, Canada M6K 3H6
Distributed in the United Kingdom by GMC Distribution Services
Castle Place, 166 High Street, Lewes, East Sussex, England BN7 1XU
Distributed in Australia by Capricorn Link (Australia) Pty. Ltd.
P.O. Box 704, Windsor, NSW 2756, Australia

For information about custom editions, special sales, and premium and corporate
purchases, please contact Sterling Special Sales at 800-805-5489
or specialsales@sterlingpublishing.com.

Printed in China
Lot #:
2 4 6 8 10 9 7 5 3 1
03/12

www.sterlingpublishing.com/kids

SILVER PENNY STORIES

WITHDRAWN
Hansel and Gretel

Told by Deanna McFadden
Illustrated by Stephanie Graegin

A woodcutter and his family came upon hard times. The woodcutter was so poor, he could no longer afford to buy food for his two children, Hansel and Gretel.

"What shall we do?" he asked his wife, the children's stepmother.

She had a plan: "Tomorrow we'll take the children deep into the woods and leave them there."

The woodcutter thought this was a wicked idea, but he could see no other way.

Hansel and Gretel overheard their parents talking about leaving them in the forest.

Gretel cried. Hansel patted his sister's shoulder.

"Hush, I'll think of something," he said.

That night, Hansel slipped outside and filled his pockets with white pebbles.

The next morning, their stepmother gave them each a stale crust of bread.

As they walked into the woods, Hansel dropped the pebbles from his pocket on the ground to leave a trail behind them.

When they reached the middle of the forest, the woodcutter gathered sticks and built the children a fire. Their stepmother said, "Now lie down and sleep. We'll come and find you when we are done chopping wood."

Hansel and Gretel sat down to eat their stale bread. The warm fire made them very tired and they soon fell asleep. By the time they woke up, night had fallen. But the moonlight guided them to their trail of pebbles and they found their way back home.

The woodcutter was happy to see his children. He had not wanted to leave them in the forest.

But his wife made him try again the next day. Hansel did not have time to gather pebbles, so he tore up the crust of bread his stepmother gave him and left a trail of bread crumbs instead.

Once again, the children fell asleep by the fire. When they woke up, they searched in the moonlight for the trail of bread crumbs. But birds had eaten them!

Lost and hungry, Hansel and Gretel wandered through the woods. On their third day in the forest, a bird called out to them sweetly. They followed the bird and came upon a little house.

"Why look!" Hansel pointed, "The walls are made of bread!"

"And the roof is made of cake!" Gretel shouted.

The children ran to the house and began to eat.

They were so busy eating that they didn't notice an ugly old woman step outside. She said, "Nibble, nibble, little mouse. Who's that nibbling at my house?"

Hansel and Gretel replied, "Just two little children who are very hungry."

The old woman said, "My dears, why don't you come inside for a meal?"

The old woman treated Hansel and Gretel to a delicious dinner. That night she tucked them into two tidy, comfy beds and showed them all her treasures. But she was only pretending to be kind. She was a wicked witch who thought Hansel and Gretel would make a tasty meal!

The next morning, the witch locked Hansel in a shed. She made Gretel cook for him day and night to fatten him up.

Finally, after many days, the witch grew tired of waiting. She ordered Gretel to boil some water.

Gretel knew that the witch planned to cook Hansel in the pot!

Then the witch said, "We must also bake a delicious dessert. You must crawl into the oven to see if it's warm."

Gretel knew that the witch planned to bake her! So she said to the witch, "I don't know how to crawl inside. Would you show me?"

The witch became angry. "Silly girl," she said. "There's plenty of room. Watch me."

When the witch poked her head into the oven, Gretel pushed her in and locked the oven door. The old witch howled. Gretel ran outside and released Hansel from the shed.

Together, they gathered up the witch's treasures and set off into the forest. The more they walked, the more familiar the woods became. Finally they saw their father's house in the distance.

When the woodcutter saw his children, he gathered them in his arms. He had felt awful after leaving them in the forest and was overjoyed to see them again. While the children were gone, their cruel stepmother had died.

Hansel and Gretel showed their father the witch's treasures, and they knew they would never be poor or hungry again.